BEN'S MONSTER

Created by Dr. Rob Cardwell

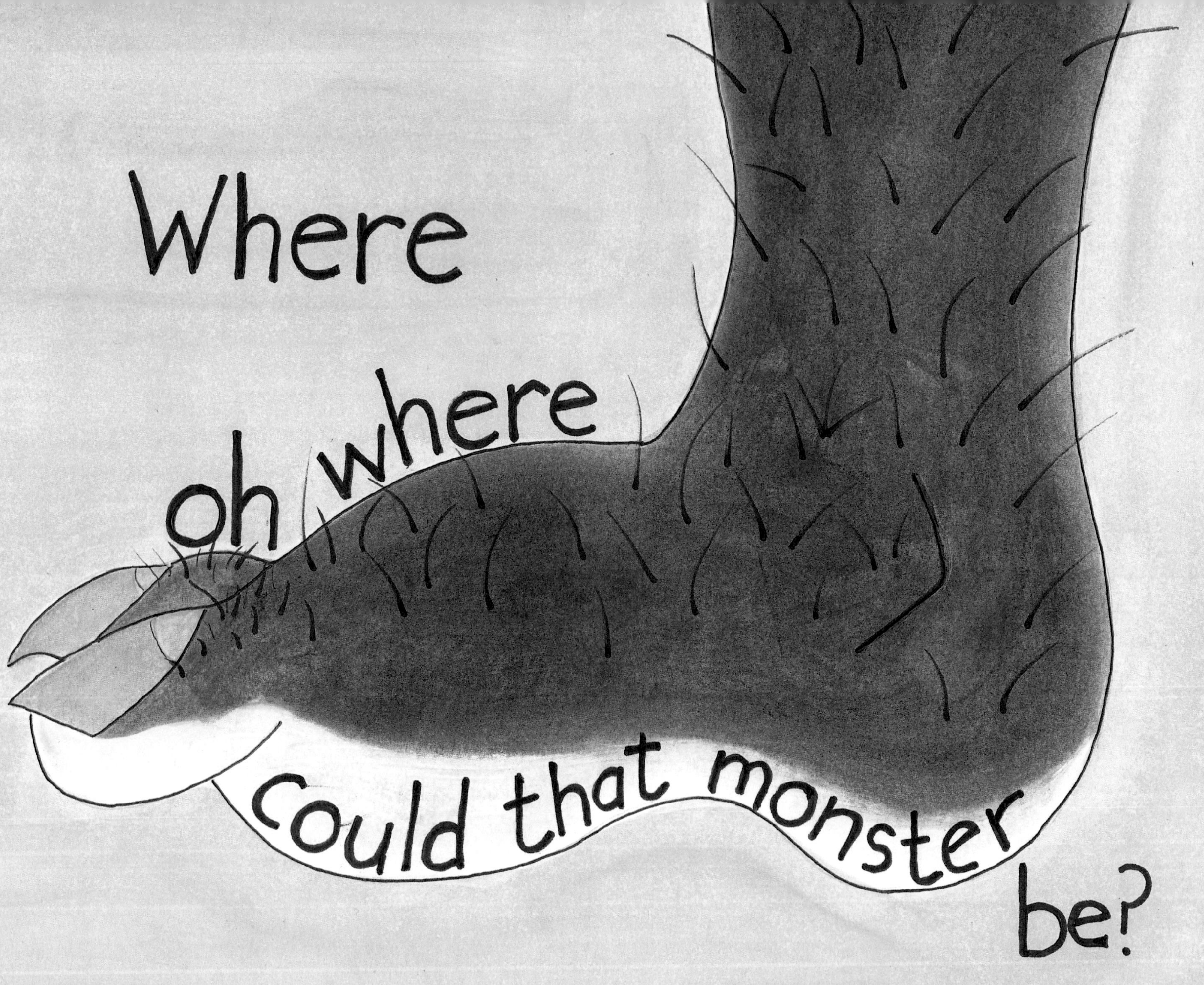
Where
oh where
could that monster
be?

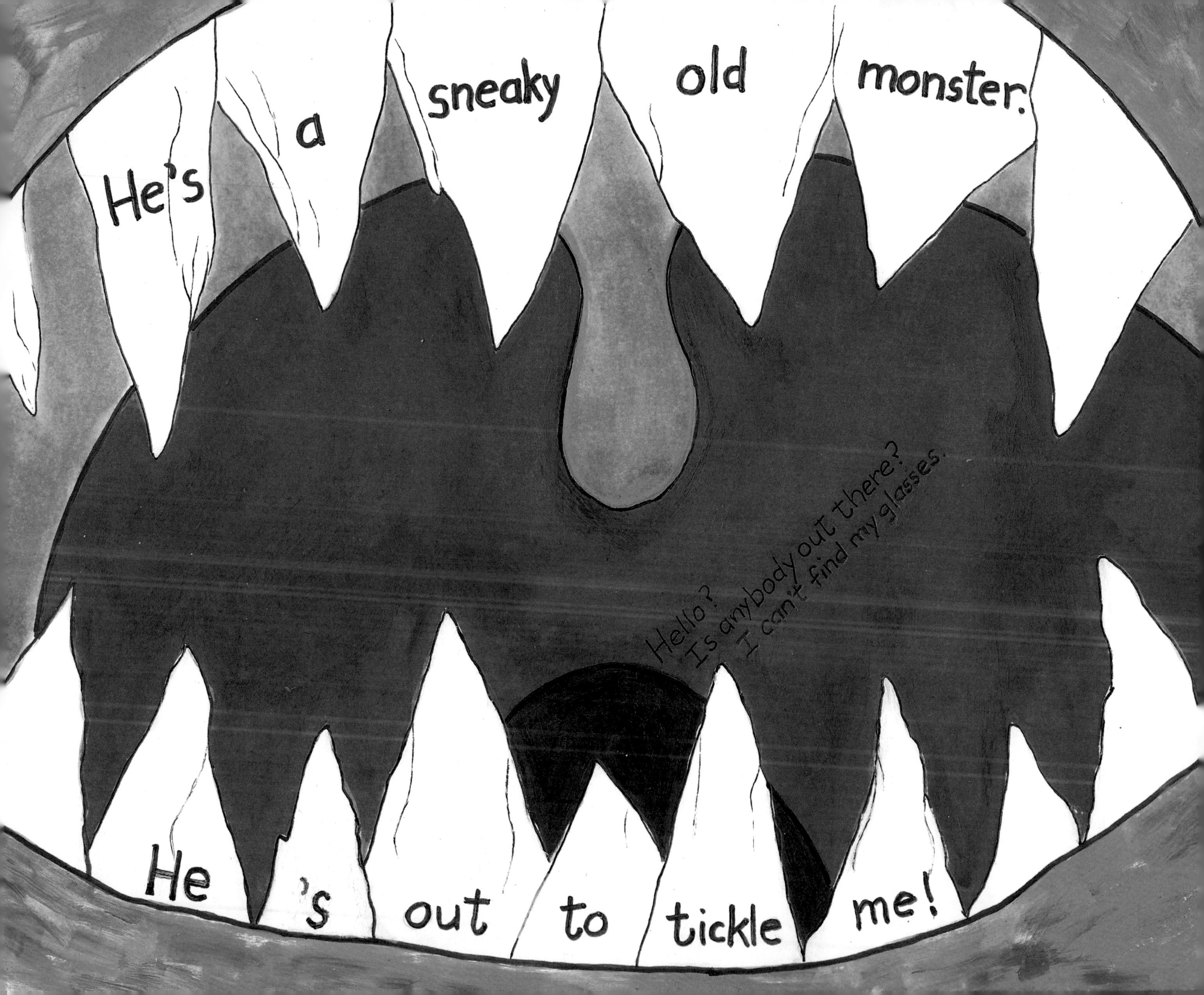
He's a sneaky old monster.
Hello? Is anybody out there? I can't find my glasses.
He's out to tickle me!

He's a ticklish monster,

I'm very ticklish

He's out to tickle me!

continued...

The closet
is dark.
A fine hiding spot.

beware of
dark closet ←

It's really
dark in here.

Open it wide!
And there he's

← To open

not.

No Monsters
Here

phew!

Under the
table?
Beneath
the
bed?
No and No!!
All this dread
in my
head!
R.I.P.

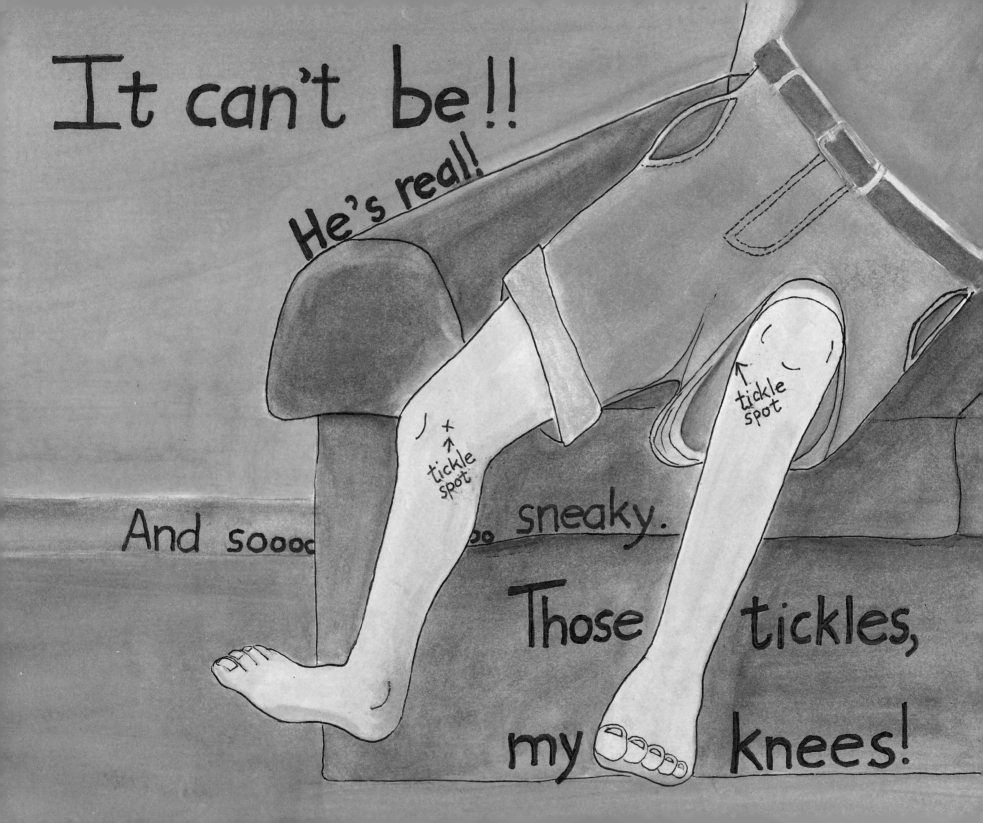

Are those footsteps in the hall?

A knocking on the wall?

Squeaks and creaks in the floor outside my door?

THUMPITY THUMP!

I can hear him breathing

He's very near. Shhh...

I can hear him breathing

Breathing in my ear.

Do I dare turn around ?

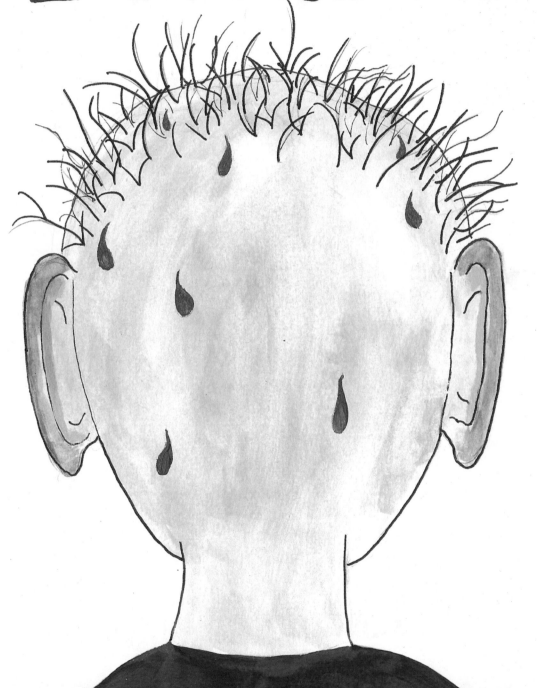

Do I dare take a look?

Oh me,
OH MY !
THE TICKLE MONSTER
IS READING
ME THIS BOOK !

To Ben

Ben's Monster

Published by: Dr. Rob Cardwell
P.O. Box 1855
Ocean City, NJ 08226

CPSIA information can be obtained
at www.ICGtesting.com
Printed in the USA
LVRC102001210322
714029LV00002B/21